Peter Cottontail™ Easter Surprises!

By Mary Man-Kong
Illustrated by Linda Karl

A GOLDEN BOOK · NEW YORK

ISBN 978-0-553-50820-8

randomhousekids.com

Printed in the United States of America

10 9 8 7 6 5 4 3 2

Colonel Wellington B. Bunny chooses Peter Cottontail
to be the new Chief Easter Bunny.

Peter Cottontail can't wait for Easter!

Peter hops to it!

Bunny Business

Peter has so much to do before Easter. Look up, down, backward, and forward to find all the things he needs to get ready for the big day.

baskets · chocolates · bonnets
eggs · jelly beans · flowers

A	S	R	E	W	O	L	F	X	C
G	N	K	X	Q	F	Q	Z	N	H
Y	A	X	N	Y	O	B	E	C	O
S	E	K	U	G	P	A	M	S	C
N	B	H	U	K	L	S	N	J	O
N	Y	Y	Z	M	Q	K	X	F	L
P	L	B	O	N	N	E	T	S	A
P	L	X	N	V	S	T	X	D	T
C	E	C	Q	B	O	S	G	G	E
Z	J	Q	N	X	V	L	P	M	S

ANSWER:

Peter checks on the Easter flowers.

There are jelly beans everywhere!

Peter collects eggs.
How many eggs can you count?

The bunnies make *egg*-cellent Easter baskets.

Time to paint the eggs!

Help Peter decorate this egg.

A bunny sculpts chocolate bunnies.

Time to check the Easter eggs!

The bunnies put flowers in the baskets.

But Peter isn't perfect. Sometimes he fibs.

Evil Irontail wants to rule April Valley.

Irontail challenges Peter to a contest.

The bunny who delivers more eggs
on Easter morning will win.

Irontail thinks he can beat Peter Cottontail.

The colonel tells Peter to get plenty of rest
before the contest.

Peter throws a big party!

Peter goes to bed very late.

Irontail gives Peter Cottontail's rooster alarm clock
bubble gum. The rooster does not crow—
it blows bubbles!

Peter sleeps all through Easter Day.

Irontail wins the contest! He wants to make
chocolate spiders for Easter.

Peter leaves April Valley and finds himself
in the Garden of Surprises.

Mr. Sassafras promises to help Peter.

Mr. Sassafras shows Peter a magical
Yestermorrow mobile.

Peter will use the Yestermorrow mobile to go back in time to Easter morning. Look at the top picture. Circle five differences in the bottom picture.

ANSWER:

Antoine the pilot takes Peter back in time to start Easter again.

Connect the dots so Peter and Antoine can fly in the Yestermorrow mobile.

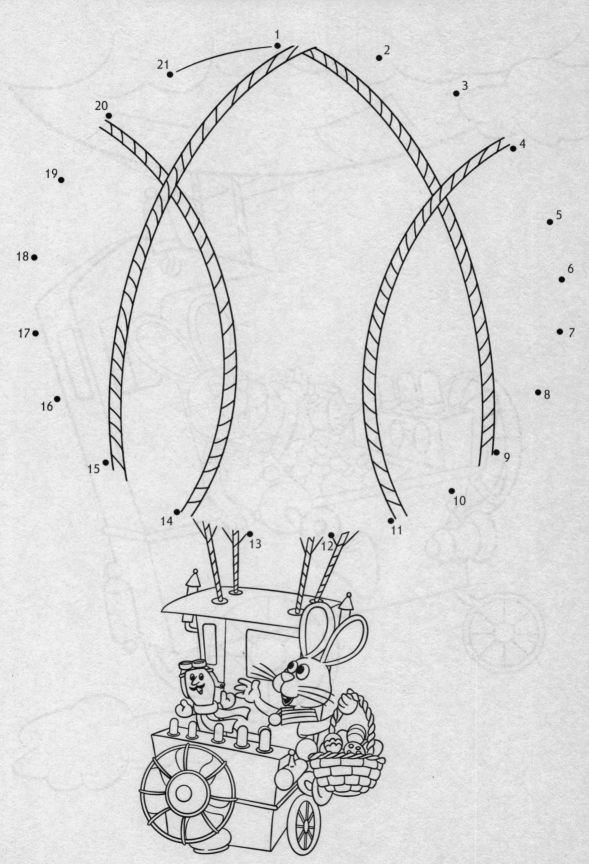

Next stop: Easter!

Irontail sends his spider to put a creepy crimp in Peter's plans.

The spider fiddles with the wires so Peter can't
go back to Easter!

The flying machine falls from the sky!

Peter lands in Mother's Day.

Peter tries to give the Easter eggs away,
but no one wants them.

Peter and Antoine land in the Fourth of July!

Peter dresses up like Uncle Sam.

Decorate Peter's egg.

Can you find the real Peter below?
(Hint: He's the one who is different.)

A

B

C

D

Peter fibs and says the eggs are special
Fourth of July fireworks.

Nobody wants Fourth of July eggs!

Peter travels to Halloween.
Decorate some spooky eggs.

Peter tries to deliver eggs to a haunted house.

Peter gives a witch a Halloween egg.

Irontail's bat steals the basket of eggs.

Peter catches the eggs.

Peter dresses up as a turkey to give eggs away
on Thanksgiving.

Irontail spies on Peter with his magic egg.

Peter lands in Christmas!

"Ho, ho, ho!"

Peter meets an Easter bonnet named Bonnie.

Irontail steals Peter's eggs!

Peter gets his eggs back and travels to Valentine's Day.

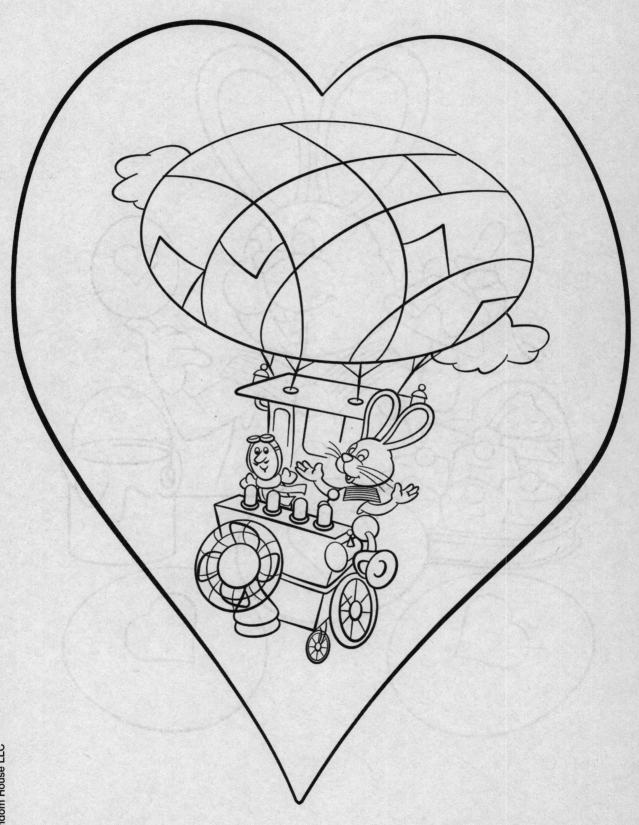

Peter makes Valentine's eggs.

Peter meets a bunny named Donna.

The two bunnies go ice-skating.

Donna hugs Peter.

Irontail wants to make sure Peter won't win the contest.

Irontail turns Peter's eggs green all the way through.

Peter has an idea! He will make shamrock eggs for St. Patrick's Day.

Peter gives out his shamrock eggs.

Peter gives out all the eggs and wins
the Easter egg contest!

Peter is the new Chief Easter Bunny!

Peter hides the Easter eggs.

Help Peter down the Bunny Trail so he can deliver the Easter eggs.

ANSWER:

Antoine turns into a beautiful butterfly.

Everyone gets ready for the Easter parade!

April Valley throws a party for Peter.

Time to celebrate!
Decorate the Easter cake.

Peter brings Donna some flowers.

Peter bakes cookies for his guests.
Decorate the cookies.

Peter and his friends have an Easter race.

The bunnies have presents for Peter.

Peter wears a funny bonnet.

Peter and Donna take a spring stroll.

This duck is ready for Easter.

Peter thinks the chick is *eggs*-tra special!

Draw some eggs to fill the Easter basket.

Peter gives everyone a picture from the party.

Enjoy this Easter with someone you love.

1. Have a grown-up help you cut out the card!

2. Fold the card in half.

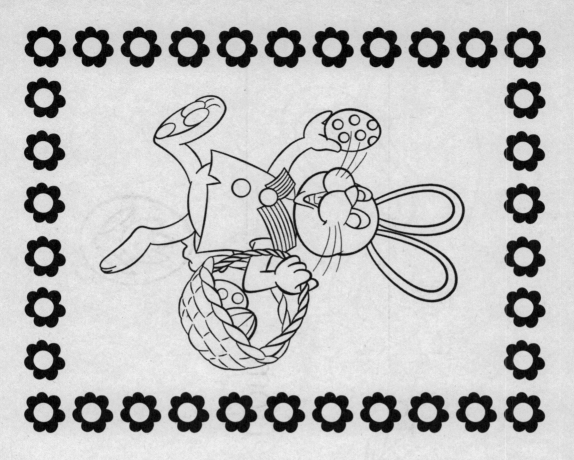

3. Fill out the card, then color and decorate it.

4. Give the card to someone you love!

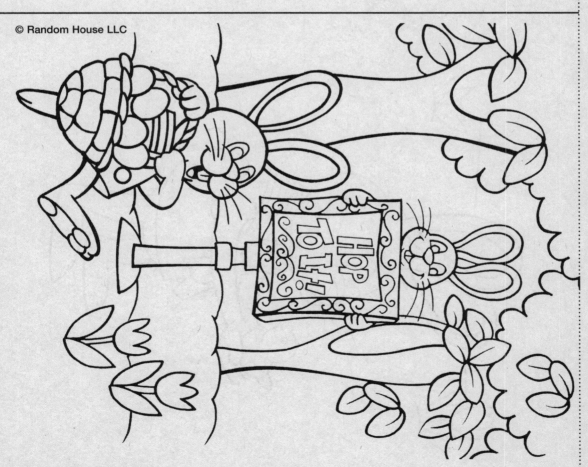

Hop To It!

To

From

Peter is off on a big Easter adventure!

Peter drops Easter eggs from the Yestermorrow mobile.

The children have fun finding the Easter eggs.
How many eggs can you count?

A little boy picks flowers for his mother.

Peter gives a girl a pretty new Easter bonnet.

Peter shares his eggs with some cute kittens.

Help Peter create an *eggs*-traordinary egg.

Donna helps Peter give out Easter eggs.

Peter hops down the Bunny Trail.